STAY IN THE GAME

THE CONTEST

00:00:01

STAY IN THE GAME

Megan Atwood

darbycreek

MINNEAPOLIS

Darby Creek
A division of Lerner Publishing Group, Inc.
241 First Avenue North
Minneapolis, MN 55401 USA

For reading levels and more information, look up this title at www.lernerbooks.com.

The images in this book are used with the permission of: © iStockphoto.com/ hartcreations (teen); © Andycash/Dreamstime.com (digital clock); © Vidakovic/ Bigstock.com (Abstract technology background); © iStockphoto.com/archibald1221 (circle background): © freesoulproduction/Shutterstock.com (game pieces).

Main body text set in Janson Text LT Std 12/17.5.
Typeface provided by Adobe Systems.

Library of Congress Cataloging-in-Publication Data

Atwood, Megan.
     Stay in the game / by Megan Atwood.
       pages cm. — (The contest ; 1)
     Summary: Desperate for money to pay for an experimental treatment that could save his ill grandfather's life, high school senior James enters a mysterious contest that will award the winner ten million dollars.
     ISBN 978-1-4677-7506-9 (lb : alk. paper) — ISBN 978-1-4677-8101-5 (pb : alk. paper) — ISBN 978-1-4677-8831-1 (eb pdf : alk. paper)
     [1. Contests—Fiction. 2. Conduct of life—Fiction. 3. Orphans—Fiction.]
I. Title.
PZ7.A8952Sr 2015
[Fic]—dc23   2015003988

Manufactured in the United States of America
1 – SB – 12/31/15

To my parents, always.

CHAPTER 1

DING. The sound of a new email woke James up. Groaning, he rolled over and looked at his phone. *2:30 a.m.* showed blurrily through the cracked screen. Way too early. Probably just junk mail. He rolled over and tried to go back to sleep. Two seconds later, though, his eyes flew open. He wondered if it was the hospital—more bad news for him and his grandpa. Or maybe someone was finally following up with him about a job application . . .

He jumped out of bed, heart pounding. He could barely see on his phone, so he moved to his ancient computer and jiggled the mouse. The screen lit up. There it was, one new message. Sent from someone named "Benefactor."

He took a deep breath. Of course it wasn't the hospital. Or any of the places he'd been applying for jobs. None of those places would send an email. Especially not at 2:30 in the morning.

Like he always did in the middle of the night, he listened for his grandpa's breathing. The hiss and hum of the oxygen machine told him things were okay. He exhaled and tried to get his heart rate down.

"Thanks a lot, Benefactor." Still, he read the first line in the email preview. He squinted to make sure he was seeing it right.

This message is for James Trudeleau, senior at Cleveland High School in East St. Paul. We have . . .

The preview cut off. James wavered between his bed and the computer desk. He could reach out an arm in either direction and touch both things. He stared at the ceiling for a minute and then gave in. He was up. He might as well read the rest of the message. It was probably just some stupid company trying to sell him something. Like he could afford to buy anything. Ever.

He said to no one, "Barking up the wrong tree, guys." But he sat back down anyway and clicked open the message. He squinted again. He really needed glasses. But that was the least of the health problems in the Trudeleau household, so he would just hold off.

This message is for James Trudeleau, senior at Cleveland High School in East St. Paul. We have a proposition for you. You have been selected to participate in a contest. We will give you ten tasks to complete. Each task is worth $1 million. If you complete all ten, you will be awarded the full $10 million. If you do not complete all ten, you will be awarded nothing. If you do not complete the ten tasks before someone else finishes the contest, you will be awarded nothing.

If you wish to participate, you can sign the contract at the website below.

James's eyes skimmed over the URL. He kept reading.

More information will be given once you sign. You have two days to decide.

We want to express our sympathy for your grandfather's illness. We understand that a new experimental treatment could save his life, but his health insurance will not cover it. Think about our offer.

The Benefactor

James sat back in the chair, sweat beads multiplying down his back. How did they know all this about him? What *was* this?

The computer screen glowed in his dark room. The only other light came from the lamppost outside the apartment building. A shadow crossed the light, and James stood up fast, almost knocking the chair over. He crawled on his bed to the window and peeked out, down two stories to the street lamp.

A figure stood by the lamppost, leaning against it. James couldn't see much except that the person wore dark pants and a dark shirt. He shivered. This person couldn't be watching him, right? This had to be just a coincidence. He was being paranoid. The email was just a scam or a prank . . .

He went to the computer again and turned it off. The ancient thing whirred and clicked like an old-time movie projector. He crawled into his bed again but couldn't resist looking out the window. Whoever had been standing there was gone, and James heaved a sigh of relief. *Just get some sleep.* With school tomorrow, he needed as much rest as he could get.

He was about to lie back down when a fluttering on the lamppost caught his eye. Some kind of banner was attached to the post. A slight breeze picked it up and showed the banner at a new angle. Now he could actually read what it said.

James. We're waiting.

James slammed his body back against the wall, heart racing yet again. Seconds ticked by. Maybe minutes. When he was calm enough, he peeked around the window again.

The banner was gone.

CHAPTER 2

After four hours of tossing and turning, James heard his grandfather's call.

"Doodle, come help me up." The hissing of the oxygen machine stuttered a little, and James knew his grandpa had sat up.

He threw on some shorts and a T-shirt and headed across the hall to his grandpa's bedroom. "Gramps, I keep telling you not to call me that."

James tried to give him his best stern look, but the twinkle in his grandpa's eye always made him smile. His grandpa said, "Who's my little doodle-ums?" And then laughed a big laugh, phlegmy and wheezy. Like all his laughs, it ended in a coughing fit. And he laughed a lot. Especially at the nickname that used to embarrass James so much.

For the past eight years, James's grandpa had managed to make him smile about just about anything. Whether James was freaking out about school or a girl or some fight he'd had with friends. And when James worried about how they'd afford next week's groceries. Or just when he was missing his mom and dad, which was practically all the time . . . his grandpa always knew how to make him smile. And to make him feel safe.

Even when he could barely breathe and was strapped into an oxygen tank.

When his grandpa's body stopped convulsing from the cough, James handed him a tissue. Bright red blood spotted it, but James pretended not to see it. Still, he felt the familiar drop in his stomach. "Gramps, you have to quit cracking yourself up."

His grandpa leaned hard on James's shoulder and stood up. "Oh, who cares about life if there's no laughter?" He put his hand on James's face and smiled big. "You're such a good boy, James. Helping an old man like me. Your mom and dad would be proud. I know you'll go far. I just wish I could be alive to see it."

His grandpa was saying things like this more often now. Big, sweeping statements about how he wouldn't be alive much longer. James didn't think he could take it. First his mom and dad, and now his grandpa? That was too unfair. Too much.

The email flashed in his mind, but he pushed the thought aside. That was clearly someone messing with him. Now rage took over. Someone awful messing with him. On top of everything else.

"Grandpa, you're going to make it."

His grandpa shook his head. "The doctor said there was a 10 percent chance, James."

"That's still a chance!" But even as he said it, James didn't believe himself. His grandpa needed that new treatment. And even that wasn't a guarantee—it had only been tried eight times in the United States. But it was better than a 10 percent chance.

And it only cost around $200,000. He couldn't even wrap his head around that number.

All of a sudden, his grandpa sat down hard on the bed again. His face was pale. "Son, you may have to call the doctor." And then, to James's horror, his grandpa passed out.

* * * * *

A few hours later, James's grandpa was settled in a hospital bed. But he still hadn't woken up. A doctor came to talk to James.

Dr. Cheng shuffled notes in front of her and didn't look James in the eye. James didn't like where this was going. He'd become an expert at reading doctor body language. Her body language said, *Things are bad*. "Is there anyone else who can come help out?"

James swallowed. "My aunt. But she's in Kenya." Seeing the doctor's surprise, he added, "She works for a medical nonprofit there. Doctors Together."

Dr. Cheng nodded. "I've heard of it. Well, you may want to get in touch with her." James waited. He dreaded what was coming.

Already his eyes burned.

"I've put in a call to your grandpa's regular oncologist. She should be on her way. But . . . " James looked away. He knew what was coming.

"There isn't much time left." The doctor put her hand on James's shoulder, and it took everything in him to not shrug it off. "I'm sorry, James. You'll want to confirm with his oncologist, but I'm guessing *maybe* six weeks."

James nodded but didn't trust his voice.

After the doctor left, James sat staring at his grandpa. He looked so . . . old. So weak.

The tears started pouring down his face. And then he ran. Out into the hall, down the stairs, then through the lobby and outside. He collapsed on the grass in a hidden corner of the lawn.

After what seemed like hours of sobbing, James managed to catch his breath. He stood up. He was tired of thinking about how horribly unfair life could be. Like his grandpa always said: *Fair is for riding horses. It doesn't do much in real life.* Time to pull himself together.

He needed to call his aunt. And the school. He took out his phone and called the school secretary. His grandpa had been a teacher at the school years and years ago, so a lot of the staff knew him. James hated the note of pity he heard in the secretary's voice, mostly because he was afraid he'd lose control again. After he finished, he dialed his aunt Beth's number. The longest of long-distance calls. She didn't answer—no surprise with the time difference. So he left a message telling her to call him back right away. Then he squared his shoulders and walked back into the hospital. He was going to be there for his grandpa, the way his grandpa had been there for James his whole life. Especially the past eight years, since his parents died.

As James walked through the lobby, he saw a computer center to his left. He stopped short. The person walking behind him almost ran into him. James said "sorry" absentmindedly and stared at the computer.

What would it hurt to look at this website? If it was a virus, he was pretty sure the hospital computers would detect it. Unlike his old computer at home. Or his phone, he suspected.

He walked slowly into the center and sat down at an empty computer. First he checked his email. He had another one from the Benefactor, this one sent at 7:00 am.

Dear James,

Login: doodle

Password: treatment

James sat back from the computer like he'd been slapped. They had to be watching him. But how? And who were they? Despite the air conditioning in the hospital, James started sweating again. He looked around. Only one guy was in the room, and he seemed focused on his own computer screen. Though at this point, James felt as if *everyone* was watching him.

Slowly, he opened a new tab and pasted the URL from the Benefactor's email.

A screen popped up: black, with only the login and password boxes on it. James entered the login and password, blushing at the login name. How had they known . . . ? He shook his head and decided to just see what would happen.

When he pressed Enter, the page dissolved. Now a chart appeared on the screen. His name was at the top of the first column. The other three column headings said "Anonymous." Under each name, the numbers 1-10 were listed down the column. Under one of the anonymous columns, the word "Completed" filled the No. 1 slot.

In James's No. 1 slot, a timer was ticking away. It read "23:58:20." He watched in fascination as the last two digits counted down. And then he understood—whatever his first task was, he had twenty-four hours to do it. Actually, he now had twenty-three hours and fifty-seven minutes.

Ten million dollars. Enough money to save his grandpa and then some. New place, nice neighborhood, maybe by a lake. College tuition . . .

A pop-up screen appeared. The box read:

You will complete each task before the timer ends for that task. If you do not complete the task in that time, the task is void, and you are out of the contest. To win the $10 million, you must finish all 10 tasks before the others in this contest do. You will be paid in cash. Tell no one about this. We will know if you do. If you do tell someone, all tasks are void and punishment is severe. You may not ask questions. You must do exactly as the task instructs. Do you agree to these terms?

Two boxes appeared under the agreement: yes and no. James needed to put an X in one of them.

James looked around the room again, remembering his grandpa's pale face. What else could he do?

And what did he have to lose?

With a shaking hand, he moved the cursor to the "yes" box. He clicked.

CHAPTER 3

The page exploded.

Or so it seemed. Colors fireworked on the screen, then swirled around the edges. The screen turned white, empty except for the timer in the right-hand corner. 23:55:41.

Words appeared as if someone were typing them out letter by letter.

TASK 1

At school tomorrow, you will deliver an anonymous note to the principal's office that says, "Maiv Moua is cheating in computer science." If you complete this task correctly, you will earn $1 million.

James sat back in the chair and rubbed his hand over his head. He didn't know what he'd thought the tasks might be, but this . . . This seemed just stupid.

He walked it through his head. This Maiv person, whoever that was, would probably be asked about the note. And then she—he?—probably she—would say she wasn't cheating. Then the school would check and find out it wasn't true.

Or—find it *was* true. In which case James would be doing a good thing.

He clicked open another tab and got on Facebook, searching for a Maiv Moua. He found four girls with the same name, but only one had Cleveland High School on the profile. The profile picture was just a photo of some flowers. He clicked on it to open up the page.

Nothing. Just a profile pic (no cover pic at all), Cleveland High School, and her name. Everything else was private. For a split second, James thought about sending her a friend request, but something stopped him.

Mostly the fact that he was about to accuse her of cheating.

James tried to ignore the uncomfortable little feeling in the back of his head. It would turn out all right. This task wasn't that bad after all.

He could do it for a million dollars, no problem.

* * * * *

James got to school early the next morning. After locking his bike up, he sat on the stairs in front of the entrance.

One million dollars. His grandpa's life.

He opened up his backpack and took out the note he'd written the night before. The envelope had the principal's name printed across it. He'd tried to disguise his handwriting. The note looked like a kindergartner had written it.

More and more people began walking by. The 8:00 bell would ring in ten minutes. He had to find a way into the principal's office without being noticed.

He got up and shouldered his backpack, holding the note crumpled in one hand. All of a sudden, James wanted nothing more than to be done with this task. He bounded up the last three steps of the entrance and almost mowed people down getting in the door.

The air conditioning of the school hit him. He breathed in. The school's air system was wildly unpredictable in each room, but the hallways were always freezing. The cool air calmed him down and made his shoulders crawl down from his neck. He loosened his grip on the note and walked to the principal's office with new purpose.

James wasn't sure how this would go. He wasn't even sure where the principal's mailbox was. But when he walked into the admin office, he walked into chaos. Two kids were fighting *in* the office. The liaison officer stood between them, glaring, and the rest of the office staff seemed to be hovering nearby or scurrying around.

The main desk was empty.

This was his chance. James put the letter

on the desk. He lingered a minute by the door, pretending to be looking at a bulletin board, until the fight was under control.

The school secretary returned to the main desk, picked up the letter, then moved toward the principal's office.

James smiled. One task down.

CHAPTER 4

By third period study hall, James could barely sit still. He had to find out if it had worked. He asked his study hall teacher if he could go to the library, and she wrote out a pass, no questions asked. She didn't even look at him as he took it from her.

He practically sprinted to the library. When he got there, he snagged a computer and looked around to make sure the librarian wasn't watching him. He typed in the URL for the contest and then his login and password.

The words he wanted popped up on the screen.

TASK 1 COMPLETE

James sat back and sighed. It was worth it. It had to be worth it. He just needed to ignore the uneasy, awful feeling poking at him. They would find out that this girl didn't actually cheat and everything would be OK. It wasn't that big of a deal.

The screen went blank, and then another timer appeared.

72:00:00.

He sat up closer to the computer. He had three days to do the next task. The writing appeared letter by letter:

Check back at 3:45 for your next task.

James slid back on his chair and gave a sigh of relief. The first task was done. Not so hard. And he had three whole days for the next one. Hope swelled through his chest. Maybe, just maybe, he could do this.

A laugh near him caught his attention. A girl and a boy sat together at a table, snickering into their hands. When James heard the name Maiv, he sat up.

"Did you hear? She was caught cheating.

She can't get the scholarship now."

The boy laughed. "Thank God. She gets everything. Little miss freaking perfect. And it turns out she was cheating this whole time!"

The girl shook her head. "Can you imagine her cheating? I can't believe she did."

The boy shrugged. "I'm just glad she finally got knocked down a peg."

The bell rang, but James sat frozen, watching the two walk out of the library.

Whoever this Maiv was, she suddenly had become real to him. And so had his actions. Whether or not she cheated—things probably weren't just going to be OK for her.

James swallowed the bile in his throat.

* * * * *

At home, James sat in his room, running his hand over his head. He couldn't stop thinking about what he'd done. And those students in the library . . . they'd been so pleased. He'd never been that guy. He had never wished bad things on people. Much less *done* anything to hurt anyone on purpose. Even when someone was being stupid or racist or just cruel to him, which happened more than he'd like to think about. It just wasn't worth it. And like his grandpa always said, "You never know what someone is going through." With his parents gone, James completely understood that.

A fresh wave of shame washed over him when he thought about what his grandpa would think. But he shook it off. James was doing this for *him*. He was saving his life.

As if he'd made it happen, his phone alarm went off for 3:45.

James jumped into the chair and logged in to the website. Like before, words began to appear on the screen as if someone were typing them out right then.

TASK 2

Go to Kenwood High School within the next three days. Go to the gym and wait until exactly 3:40. Then go into the girls' locker room. (It will be empty.) Find locker 37. The padlock combination is 23-45-05. Open the locker, take the backpack inside, and hide it at home. Make sure no one sees

you. Take the backpack to your apartment
and keep it there. Do not look in it. We will
know if you do.

James sat back in his chair like a strong
wind had hit him. This one seemed a little
sketchier than just dropping off a note. This
was actual stealing.

He stood up and paced around the very
small space of his room.

Could he actually *steal* something?

Something ticked on the computer. He saw
that one of his competitors had moved to task 3.
He would have to do this next task way before
the three-day limit if he wanted to stay in the
game. If he wanted to save his grandfather's life.

He could steal something. For his grandpa.
And anyway, it wasn't like he was stealing $10
million. He was just stealing a backpack and
earning $10 million.

James almost laughed. Finally he had a job!
Just not the kind of job he'd been hoping for.
This one was a little more . . . complicated.

His ringtone made him jerk so hard that
he knocked an old soda bottle off his desk. He

pulled out his phone and answered the call. It was his aunt.

"James?" Her voice sounded crackly and far away. "How is he doing?"

"Not good, Aunt Beth. They say maybe six weeks." There was quiet on the other end of the line. He suspected his aunt was crying.

"James, I'm trying my hardest to come home, but I'm stuck in Kenya right now. I'll call the doctor and see if we can't at least make him more comfortable."

James was proud of his aunt. She'd put herself through school to become a doctor, and now she was in Kenya helping people who needed her. James wanted to follow in her footsteps. But this was the trade-off. She hadn't been able to take care of James after his parents died. And she was stuck in the middle of a different country when something bad happened. When *he* needed her. At that moment James would've given anything to have someone else around who knew what was going on, what he was going through.

"James?" Beth's voice started breaking up.

"Yeah? I'm still here."

"Listen, I can't hear you, but if you can hear me, I'm going to make it home in the next couple of days here. I have to get my visa sorted and find a pilot who can take me to Nairobi. Sit tight, James. I'll be there soon."

The phone went silent. James thought for a second. Maybe his aunt could come up with some way to get the treatment. Maybe she had doctor friends who could help. Maybe he wouldn't have to do this contest. If she could make it back in a few days . . .

Suddenly the phone chimed, telling him he had an email. James turned back to the computer screen and pulled up his email account. Another message from the Benefactor.

Your aunt can't help. Only we can help. You have three days for the next task. Do not fail.

Sweat trickled down James's spine. He looked at his phone. Could it possibly be bugged? How did they know all these things? He didn't even know how to check for bugs. How would anyone know if he looked in the bag he was supposed to take? How did they know about Aunt Beth?

CHAPTER 5

James shifted from foot to foot. He knew he looked like he was up to something.

He *was* up to something.

He remembered his grandpa's words, all through his childhood. "Son, being a man means making the right choices. You do that for yourself. At the end of the day, you have to go to sleep knowing who you are. But you are also a young black man, so you have mountains to climb. People expect you to fail. So wouldn't it be nice to go to sleep knowing you are the man you want to be *and* you proved them all wrong?"

James swallowed down the meaning of his grandpa's words. *I'm saving his life, I'm saving his life, I'm saving his life.*

Finally, the bell rang. James checked his watch. 3:25. He took a quick peek in the windows on the building's lower level, where the gym sat. He couldn't believe how rich this school was. If he'd known, he would have worn a different pair of jeans. When he saw movement in the halls, he headed to the front doors and walked in.

He shouldn't have worried. His clothes looked just like everyone else's. He'd forgotten that rich people liked to thrift shop for fun.

He blended in with the other students, following one group after the next. If he was remembering the map from the school's website, the gym would be just around the corner where he stood. Sure enough, when he turned the corner the gym was right there.

And so was a girl. He smacked right into her. She reeled backward, landing hard on the floor. Her backpack slipped off her shoulder. She dropped her phone, and it skidded away.

James started to apologize, reaching out to help her up. But the girl didn't even seem to notice him. She lunged toward the phone. As she snatched it up, James caught a glimpse of the name monogrammed across the phone cover: *Ana*. She turned around, still on the floor, clutching the phone to her chest. Three other girls walked by and snickered at her. She didn't even notice.

James said, "Are you OK?" He got a good look at her now. She had long, dark brown hair and deep dark brown eyes. Her skin was only a few shades lighter than his. He couldn't help but notice how beautiful she was. His heart skipped a beat.

"Yeah. Fine." She stood up fast. James saw her backpack still sitting on the floor behind her. He reached for it, but she snapped it up before he could get there.

"I got it," she said, her voice curt and short. Then her face softened, and she managed a weak smile. "Sorry. Have a good day."

James watched her walk away down the hall, in the opposite way she had been going.

An orange-and-green patch on her backpack stood out against the bag's black cloth. James couldn't read the whole thing: "Something-Industries." Clearly a bag from a business. James thought that was strange in this rich school full of designer labels.

A mystery. Ana. Maybe someday he'd run into her again—less literally.

James refocused on his mission. It was already 3:30. He had to find the lockers. The *girls'* lockers. He sighed. Why'd it have to be the girls' locker room? Not only would he be a thief, but if someone caught him, he'd be branded a pervert too.

The map on the website didn't get too specific, so finding the actual locker rooms turned out to be harder than he thought. He'd just assumed they would be right by the gym. That would make sense, right? Except he took three laps around the seemingly endless hallway surrounding the gym and couldn't find anything.

He checked his phone again. 3:36.

James huffed out in frustration. Just then,

he overheard some girls talking as they walked quickly by him.

". . . Ms. Albert will be so mad if we're late. We have to change fast."

Trying to make it as smooth as possible, he turned around and followed them up a flight of stairs.

There sat the girls' locker room. The gym was so big it had two floors.

James watched as the girls rushed in. He looked left and right and then bent down to tie his shoe. His whole body shook. He knew he wouldn't be able to talk his way out of this if he was caught. He never was a very good liar.

He checked his watch again. 3:40.

He pushed open the door, listening for voices, rustling, the slam of lockers. All he heard was a drip from a faucet somewhere. The girls must have made it to their practice on time. He tiptoed in, cushioning the door so it wouldn't make any sound.

Still shaking, he read the number of the locker in the first row: 110. He had to get to 37, and of course it was on the other side of the locker room. He ducked down, though he wasn't sure what good that would do. Then he ran to the end of the room, grateful for the nice carpet on the floor. Completely different from his school. At Cleveland, everything was dingy, cold tile.

Finally, he found the locker. He stood in front of it and took a big breath. He thought of his grandpa lying in the hospital right at this moment. He thought about being alone in the apartment, no parents, no grandpa. And the sadness hit him full force.

He had to get that money. He had to.

James was no longer shaking. He twirled the combination and whipped open the door, careful to catch it before it smacked against the other lockers.

His heart leapt as he saw the backpack: black with the green-and-orange logo, which he could now fully read. *Huffmann Industries.*

This was Ana's backpack.

CHAPTER 6

James paced in the hospital corridor, desperate to get to his grandpa. After he'd sneaked out of school with the backpack, he had gotten a call from the hospital. His grandpa had been improving, but he'd fainted as soon as he stood up. Now, his grandpa's regular oncologist came out to talk to James.

"Any news on your aunt coming in?"

James chewed a fingernail and shifted from foot to foot. "She's trying to make it. She's stuck in Kenya right now."

Dr. Margolies nodded. "Yes. We talked on the phone the other day. We were both hoping to get your grandfather home so we could make him comfortable. But with this new fainting episode . . . well, I just don't think I can okay it."

Once again, James felt fear shoot through him. "Why did he faint?"

"I suspect low blood pressure." She added softly, "His body is failing, James. That's all there is to it. Our job now is to make him as comfortable as possible."

James began shifting from foot to foot again. He needed to do something. "But what about that treatment?"

Dr. Margolies shook her head. "Even if that was . . . on the table for your family . . ." *If we could afford it*, James translated in his head. "The odds aren't promising. James, I think you should prepare—"

James didn't wait to hear the rest. He walked away from her, took a deep breath, and entered his grandpa's room. It just couldn't happen. He would fix this.

The nurses looked up. His grandpa's eyes searched the room. "Beth, Jack, you guys need to clean up now." James started at the sound of his dad's name. He had never seen his grandpa like this. Clearly, he wasn't living in the present.

James turned and left the room almost as fast as he'd walked in. He took the stairs two at a time, his stolen backpack bumping against him.

He got to the hospital Internet room and slid into a chair. He had to find his next task. He would get through all the tasks faster. Before anyone else. Before anything else could happen to his grandfather. He had to win this contest.

The computer seemed to take forever to load, but finally, the contest page came up. Panic flooded through him when the counters came up. One of the contestants had gone to Task 4. His own column glowed red on Task 3. A timer came up. 48:00.

He had two days for the next one. The familiar typing began.

TASK 3

Go to Alexus Olsen High School. Spray-paint the following words in red on the low wall that leads to the front entrance. "CB, we know about your brother. His time is running out."

James closed the browser and logged off the computer. The time for thinking things through was over. He couldn't afford to be sorry for stealing Ana's backpack. He couldn't afford to worry about some girl who may or may not have cheated. And he couldn't care less about this CB person's brother.

His grandpa was all that mattered. James would graffiti the school tonight.

* * * * *

James heard the clink of the spray-paint cans in his backpack. It reminded him of an Edgar Allen Poe story he once read for English class, "The Tell-Tale Heart." Every clink of the can reminded him that this was the second time in one day he'd be doing something illegal. And, well . . . if he was honest, just wrong.

He pedaled faster. Riding his bike from East St. Paul all the way over to North Minneapolis was no small trip. And not totally safe either at 1:30 in the morning. Not safe from people in the neighborhoods and not safe from cops.

After what seemed like hours, he finally arrived at Olson High School. The outside looked a lot like Cleveland High—a little crumbly, definitely old, but not too bad. Nothing like Kenwood, but that was private, so of course it was on another level.

He parked his bike in the bushes across the street and ducked down. He could see security cameras near the school entrance. He'd expected that. He reached into his backpack and took out the plastic bag that held the spray-paint cans. Then he tucked his backpack under the bush and tried to cover up his bike as well as he could.

As he sprinted to the wall, the clinking of the cans barely registered over the roaring in his ears. He didn't see anyone around, so he dropped the cans with a loud clink and grabbed one. He'd brought two in case one failed.

Trying to hold the can steady, he wrote in huge letters: *CB, we know about your brother. Time is running out.*

The red paint dripped down, making the message creepy. James paused for a second and really looked at the words. What had he just written? Did he just threaten someone's life?

Before he could think more about it, he heard movement across the street. James whipped around and saw that someone was standing by his bike. Someone tall and muscular, probably a guy. That was all James could see at this distance. Other than the fact that this person had James's backpack slung over his shoulder.

"Hey!" James yelled, sprinting across the street. But before he could get there in time, the guy rode off on James's bike. James ran faster, but the guy was going downhill. There was no way for James to catch him. James ran all the way to the bottom of the hill. Then he put his hands on his knees and tried to catch his breath.

He looked back at the school. He'd left the paint cans there . . .

Something caught his attention near the spray-painted words. Some movement or rustling. He felt exposed. *Leave the cans—time to get out of here.* After all, he was going to have a long walk home.

James crossed the street and didn't look back again till he'd put an entire block between him and the awful words he'd just written.

CHAPTER 7

James woke up and groaned. His feet had blisters and his legs ached. The three-hour walk home had just about done him in. Last night he'd been too tired to even check the contest website.

James forced himself to sit up, shut off his alarm clock, then swung out of bed. He'd gotten exactly two hours of sleep. He limped to his computer, pulled up the website, and waited for the next task to appear. Instead the clock said 34:38.

What? He refreshed the computer.

34:24.

He sat back in disbelief. He'd completed

the task. He'd done what they'd asked. There couldn't be anything wrong with the website because the clock was still running. Still, he shut off his computer and rebooted it, waiting for the ancient machine to stop whirring and come back alive.

He pulled up the website again.

33:46.

James threw his mousepad against the wall. How could they have missed it? If they knew everything, like they seemed to, how could they not know what he did last night?

He paced around his tiny room. There was nothing on the website that would let him ask questions. No one to talk to. His whole body tensed in frustration. This had to work. He couldn't be doing this for nothing. He had to take some time to calm down and find a solution.

He stomped into the bathroom and looked at himself in the mirror. Huge bags under his eyes made him look ten years older. His face was pale, his hair getting long. He had a five-o'clock shadow. He looked awful.

He took a deep breath, then got out his

shaving kit. After he'd shaved his face and trimmed his hair, he took a long hot shower. By the time he got out, he felt human again. Though the thought of all the things he'd done still hovered in the corner of his mind. He was wrapping a towel around himself when he heard a ding from his phone: a new email. He sat down at the computer and opened it.

You did not follow directions for your latest task. You did not write the exact message given to you. This failure has been discussed with our team. Because you have done everything else correctly for this task, you are not disqualified from The Contest. But you have been docked time. You must wait ten more hours before your next task is revealed. Check back at 5:00 p.m. for your next task. Another punishment awaits you at a different time.

This is your only warning. If you fail at any other assigned task, you will be disqualified.

James stared in disbelief. He'd done everything just right. He knew he had. He racked his brain for how he could have done something wrong. Sitting back, he closed his eyes and tried to remember the task.

He'd been told to graffiti, "CB, we know about your brother. His time is running out." He was positive that was it. But he hadn't been paying total attention to the spray painting, because he'd been so worried he would get caught. Had he left something out? He could picture the words forming, the movements his arm had made . . .

His eyes flipped open. He'd forgotten the word *his*. For that, he was almost disqualified. Whoever the Benefactor was, he wasn't messing around.

James sighed. He didn't want to admit it, but he was relieved to still be in the contest, even though the other "punishment" was still out there. For now, though, there was nothing he could do until 5:00 pm. He'd go to school, visit his grandpa, then make sure that he would do exactly what he was told to do for the next task. No matter what.

CHAPTER 8

At school, James could barely keep his eyes open. He nodded off completely in history class and was rewarded with his teacher making fun of him. He couldn't even muster the outrage to make fun of him back. His algebra teacher took him aside and asked him if he was OK. All James could do was nod. After an eternity, the final bell rang and James went to his locker.

He twirled the combination and tried to remember which books he'd have to bring home for homework. He'd have to walk all the way home carrying them in his arms, since he had no bike and no backpack . . . He opened up his locker and blinked.

A folded note, with *JAMES* written in huge block letters, sat on the shelf. In his locker. The locker no one was supposed to know the combination to.

James snatched up the note and opened it.

You have been punished. We trust you will do the right thing next time.

Right then, James's phone rang. The school didn't allow students to talk on their phones in the hall, but James was terrified that the news was about his grandpa.

He grabbed the phone out of his pocket and checked to see who it was. Aunt Beth.

"I'm on my way, James." Her voice was clear and un-crackly, and the sound of it made James relax with relief.

"You were able to get away from the job? Figure out your visa and everything?"

There was a pause at the other end. And then she said, "Well, sort of. My visa's been revoked. I just got fired. They're kicking me out of the country."

James's heart clenched.

He was being punished.

At 5:00, James sat in front of his computer and bounced his knee, thinking about the conversation he'd had with his aunt. She'd been fired out of nowhere. No warning, no cause. She said she was going to appeal, but she couldn't for the life of her understand what had happened. Neither could James.

The flip side was she could get back to her dad and to James sooner.

She'd tried to sound brave about it. "Don't worry, hon. People need doctors. I'll find something else. And there are some things about this company that are just weird. I was thinking of quitting anyway so I could be closer to home. This just makes things faster. I can't wait to get there and squeeze you!"

James knew that was true. She often said she wanted to come back. But the work she did felt so important where she was.

There was no way around it. This was his fault.

What he couldn't understand was *how* the

Benefactor did it. How could he—they—it—
have that much pull? Enough to get someone
fired halfway across the world?

James shook off his questions as the clock
flipped to 5:00. He pulled up the contest
website. A new timer was up.

72:00.

The person who was on task 4 seemed
stuck, though. And now James was tied with the
other two people, whoever they were. He had a
chance. The words scrawled across the page.

TASK 3 COMPLETE

Task 4

Go to Burnett's Hardware. In the back
room, there is a file cabinet. Open the
drawer labeled H-M and take the folder
labeled "Insurance." Keep it at your home
with the backpack.

James sighed and shook his head. Was it just
him or were these tasks getting harder? But not
doing them . . . well, his aunt had paid a price
for his stupidity. He couldn't let that happen to
his grandpa too.

He thought of his grandpa. The tubes in his nose. His grandpa's gravelly voice and wheezy, contagious laugh.

He'd do just about anything to keep that laugh in this world.

CHAPTER 3

Burnett's Hardware was a tiny store scrunched
between two other tiny stores in North
Minneapolis. The windows had bars. Sales signs
in neon splashed across the windows. When
James walked in, a bell rang.

A tired-looking woman came out through
a door behind the counter. She smiled warmly
at James. "Can I help you find something?"
James immediately liked her. But behind her
he could see a door she'd just come through.
This had to be the office he needed to get
into. A pang of guilt shot through him—a
now-familiar feeling.

He said, "I'm looking for a bag. Like a backpack or a messenger bag or something. Do you carry those?"

She nodded and smiled. "We sure do. Come on back here." She led him down a row filled with school supplies. Several backpacks and other types of bags lined the walls, plus paper and pencils and notebooks. James couldn't help it, he had to ask. "How come you have school supplies at a hardware store?" He quickly covered up and said, "I mean, I was hoping you did, but I wasn't expecting it."

The woman beamed. "Well, I have two kids. So we've always stocked a few school supplies." Her smile turned sad. "It was my husband's idea, actually. He died years ago, but I still keep this up. Even though one of my kids is grown and the other is almost there . . ." She seemed to remember James and brightened up again. "Here you go! I hope you find one you like."

James's shoulders dropped. He was going to steal from a nice lady whose husband had died. This seemed way too personal. He wasn't sure he could go through with it.

At least he could buy a backpack. He grabbed the cheapest one and walked to the register. The lady seemed surprised. "Well, that was quick!" She gave him that huge smile again.

He shrugged and smiled back. "I really need a bag." He eyed the office door directly behind her. How was he going to get in there anyway? He just didn't think he could get through this task.

Just then, the sound of glass breaking startled him out of his thoughts. The lady frowned and said, "Just a minute," and then ran to the back of the store.

James tensed. It was now or never.

He ran around the counter and slipped through the door to the office. He found the file cabinet right away. As quietly as he could, he grabbed the file that said "Insurance" and ran back out. He put it in the backpack. Just as he finished zipping it, the lady came back. She looked shaken.

"Hey, are you OK?" James asked, genuinely worried. Her warm smile had vanished. Worry lines took over her expression, and there were tears in her eyes.

"One of my kids . . . has been getting threats. Never mind. Just small-minded people doing small-minded things." She wiped her eyes. "You know, a lesser person than you would have just run out of here with the backpack. I'm so glad there are still good people in the world."

James's face burned with shame. He gave her the money for the backpack and then walked out the door with his head hanging.

* * * * *

"You are such a man now!" Aunt Beth hugged James so tightly he couldn't breathe. And he didn't care. A huge weight had been lifted off his shoulders. His aunt was here. He wasn't alone.

He laughed and then picked her up. She laughed back. "No fair. You're not allowed to grow up so fast." Her laugh lines crinkled as she spoke to him. James hadn't even known how heavy he'd felt until she came.

The thought of all the things he'd done

sparked through his head, but he shook it off. His aunt was home.

"I talked to the hospital during my layover. They say Dad is doing better. We're going to set him up at home and look after him. Are you up for that? We'll go tonight and get him, OK?"

James nodded. He would be in good hands with Beth. She walked into the kitchen and started looking through the cabinets. James sat down. He hadn't realized how tired he was either.

"We need to make a grocery run soon," Aunt Beth muttered as she rummaged. But she came out with some pasta and sauce and then found some hamburger in the freezer. "Well, this will do for tonight. But we're getting vegetables in you one way or another very soon."

Suddenly, James felt like crying. "Aunt Beth . . ." He didn't even know where to start. His grandpa was sick. His parents were gone. And he'd done things in the last few days that he wouldn't have thought he was capable of.

How many people's lives had he messed with?
How could he ever come back from that?
Maybe his aunt would know what to do.

But shame spiraled through him. He couldn't
tell her what he'd done. He had acted like a
horrible person. He *was* a horrible person.

He realized she was staring at him.
He cleared his throat. "I'm just really glad
you're home."

She smiled and tears shone in her eyes. "Me
too, James. It's going to be all right."

James wasn't so sure.

CHAPTER 10

James watched the familiar font start its crawl across the page. He chewed on a hangnail and bounced his knee.

TASK 4 COMPLETE

TASK 5

You will find a jump drive outside your apartment door, in your grandfather's left shoe. Tomorrow evening, go to 45235 University Avenue. Go to the desk of Sandra Bravo. At exactly 4:50 p.m., upload the file from the jump drive onto her computer. Then take the drive with you.

Failing to do this exactly will result in failure of The Contest.

James rubbed a hand over his face. Now that Aunt Beth was here, this felt more complicated. He loved that she was home, but it made everything he had done and everything he had to do seem that much worse.

He got up and walked out to the front door of the apartment. His grandpa's shoes that had been sitting outside the door so long they had dust on them. The jump drive was wedged into the heel of the left one.

James wondered how long the drive had been in there. It could have been placed any time. He didn't even want to know what was on it.

He shut the door and slipped the drive into his pocket. Then he walked into his grandpa's room, now outfitted with a hospital bed and an oxygen machine. The machine whirred, and James watched as the saline solution dripped in the IV bag. He followed the IV line to his grandpa's wrinkled hands. Gramps looked small. Small and weak. James knew he was dying.

He felt an arm around his shoulder and his aunt said, "He looks peaceful now, don't you think?"

James shrugged off her arm, suddenly angry. "He looks awful!"

Aunt Beth said, "Shhhhh."

James laughed—a kind of laugh he'd never heard come out of his mouth. It was more than just angry. It sounded cruel. "Yeah, *shhhh*. I wouldn't want to wake the dead, right? You've given up on him!"

His aunt tried to grab his arm, a confused look on her face. "James, what's gotten into you?"

"It's just always up to me, that's all. It's always up to me." James turned around and marched to his room. He grabbed his backpack and stormed out the door before his aunt could stop him.

CHAPTER 11

James had managed to avoid his aunt for a day and a half. He knew she was confused. One minute he couldn't stop hugging her. The next minute he was yelling at her. James felt like he was losing his mind. It didn't help that he was getting absolutely no sleep.

At 4:40, he walked into the storefront building at 45235 University Avenue. The place looked well kept but small, about the size of Burnett Hardware.

He'd gone this far. He might as well keep going. His grandpa wasn't even conscious, and he'd pushed his aunt away. All he really had left was the hope of winning this contest.

The jump drive was in his pocket. A couple of times the night before, he'd almost plugged it into his computer to see exactly what he was delivering. But each time, he'd remembered that the Benefactor had somehow gotten his aunt fired.

He told himself it was probably just spyware. Nothing terrible. But the little voice in the back of his head kept poking him about it.

Still, he tamped that down and headed for the glass doors in front of him.

The name of the company was on the doors.

EarthWatch
Imagining a Better Tomorrow
through Innovation Today

The logo was a person-shaped outline with a thought bubble that held the earth inside it.

"Can I help you?" asked the receptionist.

He'd rehearsed what he was going to say the whole way over. "I'm here to see Sandra Bravo?" His voice didn't even waver.

The receptionist smiled. James gave his most

innocent smile back. He knew he looked fairly harmless. He was wearing his best khakis and a sweater with a button-up shirt underneath. Church clothes, back when his family used to go.

"Can I tell her what this is about?"

"Um, yeah, my science project is about the environment, and I called and made an appointment to interview her?"

The receptionist frowned. "I don't have you down here . . ."

James put on a distressed look. "I called a week ago? It's really important that I talk to her. This project is 60 percent of my grade."

The receptionist held up her finger and picked up the phone. "Sandra, I have a . . ." She looked at James expectantly and he said, "Jack Price." The receptionist continued, "A Jack Price here for an interview."

After a few "mm-hmms" and "uh-huhs," the receptionist pointed him back toward Sandra Bravo's office. "She's down the hall, second door on your right. She has to head out right at five today, but if you can make it quick, she'll make some time for you."

James thanked her and walked back to the office. He checked his watch. 4:45. He was almost there. And he'd have five tasks done.

A youngish woman sat clacking away at her computer. The desk faced her office door, and two chairs sat in front of it. Her hard drive was nowhere to be seen. James assumed it sat under her desk. He had five minutes to figure out how to put the file on her computer.

Seeing him enter, Sandra Bravo put her hand out and smiled. "Hello! Please take a seat." She was wearing a T-shirt with the words *Solar Power Hero* on it. Her long dark hair was tucked behind her ears.

James felt his stomach clench. Another person he was about to hurt.

"How can I help, Jack?" He flinched when she said his fake name. His dad's name. He swallowed.

"Um, I'm supposed to do an interview for a class project." His voice cracked. So much for the smooth operator he'd been when he walked in. He glanced at his watch: 4:47. He had three minutes. Sweat started at his temples.

She looked at him curiously. "What kind of project? Is your class learning about solar energy?"

"Um, yeah." He was so glad she'd given him a clue. He hadn't thought far enough ahead to come up with a fake school project. He was really no good at this spy stuff.

"Great! This is an exciting time for us. As I'm sure you know, we're a think tank that helps companies design Earth-friendly products. I truly believe we're on the eve of a breakthrough. And if it works out, solar energy is going to be easier to get, more affordable than oil or even natural gas, and sustainable for the long term." Her eyes sparkled. James felt caught up in her enthusiasm.

"That sounds amazing," he said. He didn't really follow all of it, but "easy" and "affordable"—who wasn't on board with that?

Sandra Bravo grinned. "Well, I can't say too much about specific projects. Any information we give out before a product is built could hurt the company. But I'm happy to answer general questions about what we do.

Or we can talk about successful projects we've worked on in the past."

His watch ticked to 4:49.

"Um," was all he could say. He had no idea how to get her away from her computer.

The ring of her phone startled them both. Ms. Bravo said, "Hold on one sec." Then, into the phone, she said, "What? Just a minute." When she hung up, she was no longer smiling. "Excuse me . . ." And then she stormed out of the room.

James's watch ticked to 4:50.

He took one quick look out the office door to make sure no was watching. Then he pushed the door almost all the way closed. He stepped around the desk and squatted down. Sure enough, her hard drive sat on the floor. James got down on his knees, pulled the drive forward, and put the jump drive in the USB slot.

He stood up so quickly that he almost fell over. But he righted himself and stared at the computer. Luckily, it hadn't locked up, so he wouldn't need a password. He found the jump drive icon on the desktop and opened it. It held one file called "SolarStar Share." There wasn't time to find out what it was. He ejected the jump drive and scooted around to the other side of the desk, ready to sit down again. And then he thought, *What am I doing?* He had to go. Now.

James opened the door and peeked around. A crowd of people seemed to be gathered in an office down the hall. He could slip out with no one noticing.

James edged past the front desk and opened the outside door. He took one last peek at the people in the office. Sandra Bravo was holding her hair like she going to tear it out, her face blank with shock.

James left the building.

CHAPTER 12

"I'm not hungry!" James yelled. His stomach grumbled in protest. But he needed to check his computer.

His aunt Beth opened the door. "I'm getting a little sick of this attitude, James. You're going to come down to eat in five minutes or you don't eat at all, you understand?"

Dark circles underlined his aunt's eyes. James wrestled with conflicting emotions. He was irritated by the interruption, but he knew how hard things were for her.

His irritation won. "Then I won't eat at all." He turned away from her. With a heavy sigh, she closed the door. The sound of his grandpa's whirring machines echoed through the room.

James pulled up the website.

TASK 5 COMPLETE

TASK 6

At exactly midnight tonight, call the number programmed into the phone given to you. Say, "We will come after your family." Then hang up.

At 12:30 tomorrow afternoon, wear the clothes given to you and follow this man from the Government Center office in downtown Minneapolis until he returns to the same building.

A photo loaded onto the page. It showed a thin, balding white man. He looked like every middle-class white man James had ever seen. Probably in his forties. The picture seemed to be a professional photo from a website. The guy was dressed like a lawyer in a police procedural. James tried hard to memorize his face. Then the photo vanished. James refocused on the rest of the instructions.

What phone? What clothes? For the millionth time, he wondered what he was doing with this contest. Even if these instructions made sense, they still rolled two tasks into one. The Benefactor seemed to change the rules whenever he wanted. Not that James could do anything about that. It was clear that the Benefactor pretty much did *whatever* he wanted.

At least tomorrow was Saturday. He wouldn't have to miss class again for this contest. James had always been a straight-A student. But with so much else on his mind, he was pretty sure he'd fail some classes this semester.

He turned off the computer and lay down on his bed, his arm flung over his eyes. Maybe he could forget this one. He was so tired. He could just give up now and wait with his aunt for his grandpa to die.

Without warning, tears streamed down his temples. But a knock at the door made him quickly sniff and wipe his eyes. Too late—his aunt walked in. When she saw the tears on his face, she set down the package she was holding. Then she sat on the bed with him, putting her arms around him. Before he could help it, he put his arms around her and sobbed. It felt so good to just surrender. He could feel her shaking and crying too.

When the two broke apart, his aunt smiled at him through her tears. "This is all unfair, James, I know." James briefly wondered if she could read his mind. "But we have each other. We'll get through this. You're strong and wonderful. You always have been." And she stood up. "Tacos downstairs when you're ready." James wiped his eyes and smiled back up at her. He nodded.

As she left his room, she pointed to the package she'd left on his computer desk. "Oh, this was in the lobby. It's for you."

James's heart sank.

CHAPTER 13

James wasn't surprised to find that the package contained a burner phone, a hoodie, a baseball cap, and sunglasses. As usual, the Benefactor had held up his end of this arrangement. Now it was James's turn.

The call at midnight was easy. He didn't even have to talk to a person. And he tried not to listen too closely to the pleasant, deep voice that recited the voicemail message: "Hi, this is Paul. I can't answer my phone right now, but leave a message . . ." James *had* left the message, trying to make his voice sound as deep as possible. And trying hard not to think about what he was doing.

Following Paul the next day turned out to be fairly easy too. Almost fun. With the hat and sunglasses, James felt like a spy, only without the cool equipment. At 12:30, the guy walked out of the building, and James stayed two or three people behind him.

Still, James noticed the guy noticing him. For a minute or two, James was scared—what if he called the police? But then James thought about the Benefactor. Anyone mixed up with him probably wouldn't call the police. For the first time since the Contest started, James felt a surge of power. But one look at the guy's scared face, his body language of fear, and James felt bad again. How could somebody feel good about doing things like this?

And then that feeling of power turned to rage again. How could the *Benefactor* live with himself? He had to be seriously messed up. Evil.

Paul ducked into a coffee shop, came out with a sandwich, and circled back to his office. James was pretty sure he'd spoiled the poor guy's appetite. And now James didn't know what to do with himself. He had a restless energy. He

walked to the downtown library and used the
bathroom to change out of the clothes. Then he
went to the computer terminals.

TASK 7

You will receive an envelope this afternoon.
Do not open it. At 8:00 p.m., deliver it to the
mailbox of 4201 Summit Avenue.

He was more than halfway through now.
And he was way ahead of one of the other
competitors—the one who'd been beating him.
In fact, he was in the lead.

He just wasn't sure if that was a good thing.

* * * * *

That evening, a bubble envelope was waiting
for James when he got home. James shrugged
off dinner, telling his aunt he'd eat at a friend's
house. He crammed the envelope into his new
backpack and went to catch the bus.

James took the bus all the way to Summit
Avenue, a super-rich part of St. Paul. He'd
always wondered who lived in these huge
mansions. When he got to the right house,

it was 7:45, fifteen minutes early. The house sprawled in front of him, all brick, with a manicured lawn. James was afraid of not doing exactly as he was told, so he figured he should wait. He walked to the end of the block and sat by a bus stop there, holding the envelope. He felt through the paper to see if he could figure out what it was. The objects were rectangular and stiff. They felt like printouts of photos.

He glanced around out of habit and didn't see anyone. It occurred to him that even if the Benefactor was watching him right now, it must be from a distance. James's house might be bugged, but a random bus shelter? Not likely. So if he was careful . . . maybe he could look at those photos.

James reached into his backpack. Without taking the envelope out of the bag, he carefully pried open the top and brought out about five pictures.

The photos looked like they were taken from far away and like the people in them didn't know they were being photographed. James flipped through them. A little girl about three years old, sitting on a swing, and a boy just a bit older, was pushing her. Another one: a woman pushing a stroller with the little girl in it, the boy walking alongside it. And one of a man—Paul—plus the woman and the two kids, all piling into a minivan.

James's skin was crawling. What kind of a game was this?

The alarm on his watch went off: 7:55.

James stood up and walked slowly to the house. Suddenly, all of this felt very real and very dangerous. If he got caught, how could he possibly explain himself? These were pictures of *kids*. This looked like stalking, or a threat, or blackmail. And it probably *was* all of those things.

Anyway, how could he live with himself if he went through with it? He tucked the pictures back in the envelope and put it inside his jacket. He couldn't do this to this family. Even if that meant losing the contest, losing his grandpa . . .

A voice behind him startled him. "You work here, huh?" James turned around to see a kind-looking white woman standing next to him. She had some sort of accent. "I work over there." She pointed to a huge mansion across the street. "I hope your people treat you nice," she said. "Mine aren't very nice, but it's a job anyway. Rich people—what can you do?" Then she crossed the street. James watched her walk all the way to the back of the house.

Rich people. People who could afford treatments. People who could afford to hire someone like that woman. Someone like him. And of course that woman had just assumed James was working here, not living here. The usual assumptions and prejudices.

Anger surged through him. He bounded up the steps to the house. Before he could think about it more, he dropped the pictures through the mail slot.

His watch blinked to 8:00.

CHAPTER 14

The familiar scrawl began on his phone screen. He could barely see it through the screen's enormous crack, but it was enough to make him smile.

TASK 7 COMPLETE

TASK 8

Take the next package you receive to the Amtrak station. Put it in locker 235. The combination is 85-05-42. Do not look inside the package.

If he squinted, he could just make out the clock on the website homepage. 24:00. He had a full day to complete this. No problem. He was so close, he could taste it. He took a bus home and got there at 9:00. Walking into the apartment, he said, "Anything left for dinner?"

His aunt Beth jumped at the sound of his voice. "James! I thought you ate at your friend's place?"

He stopped short. He'd completely forgotten about his lie.

"Um, I didn't like what they were having."

She narrowed her eyes. Then she pointed to the couch, where another box sat. "You have another package here." She looked away and said, fake-casually, "You're not in any trouble, are you?"

James scooped up the package and grinned. "I'm building a really slow nuclear device."

Aunt Beth grinned back. "Smart aleck. That's enough from you, then."

He put his backpack on and started back toward the door. If he could knock this task out tonight too . . . well, he'd be way ahead.

"Where are you going now?"

James thought fast. "Well, actually, this

box is for a school science project. My partner and I have been waiting for it. I'm going to go over to her house and see if we can finish the project now."

His aunt raised her eyebrows. "Her?"

James looked down and smiled. "Her name is Ana." He remembered the beautiful girl from the school and a familiar pang of guilt shot through him. He wondered what he had stolen from her.

Then he forced a smile. "See you later, Aunt Beth."

But his aunt was still giving him the hairy eye. "Uh-uh. It's after nine, James. You have school in the morning. This project can wait till tomorrow. You stay here. Sit with your grandpa. Hang out with your aunt."

James thought about arguing, then changed his mind. He *should* spend some time with his grandpa. Besides, his whole body ached with tiredness. And he was so close already. He was even ahead of schedule.

"Okay, sure." He flopped on the couch, taking off his backpack. "So what do we have for dinner?" He grinned at his aunt. "Nuclear scientists need their strength, you know."

His aunt looked at him worriedly. "Well, you sure look like you do. You've lost a lot of weight, James. You're looking scrawny."

He tried to laugh it off. "Thanks a lot." She just looked at him more intently.

"What's in the box, James?"

"Ah, nothing, just science-y stuff." His voice was light, relaxed. But he could tell his aunt didn't believe him. He'd never been much good at lying. Until now, he hadn't ever needed to be.

CHAPTER 15

The next day, James had no trouble planting the cardboard box in the locker. The train station was practically empty. James was in and out in five minutes.

Now he found himself on University Avenue again.

He'd just completed his eighth task. Only two more to go. Exhaustion settled in his bones. Flashes of the faces of people he'd harmed ping-ponged in his mind. The kids in the picture. The woman in the hardware store. Sandra Bravo.

As if he'd conjured up the business, he

found himself standing outside the EarthWatch building. The office was dark.

The buzz of an unfamiliar phone snapped James out of his trance. He remembered he still had the burner phone from when he'd called and left the eerie message for that man, Paul. He dug in his backpack and found it. A new text message had just come through.

Check the website. You have two tasks left. Once you finish these, you will win $10 million.

James pocketed the phone, frowning. He should have been happy. But all he felt was anxious and guilty.

The weight of all his choices crashed down on him. This contest was the furthest thing from a game. And it went against everything his grandpa had ever taught him.

Everything about this was wrong, he knew that now. He was just so far into it that he had no idea how to get out.

He had to tell his aunt. She'd know what to do.

Time to face things like a man.

* * * * *

When James got home, he found Aunt Beth
wringing her hands on the couch. A man he
didn't know walked out of his grandpa's room,
in scrubs. James's heart dropped.

"Is he . . .?" He couldn't even get out the
words.

"Sit down, honey." James sank onto the
couch, hearing his heart pounding in his ears.

But then Aunt Beth's face broke into a
huge smile. "Some angel has sent us a stopgap
measure to help Dad fight a little."

James sat up straight. "You mean the
treatment—"

"It's not the full treatment. But it's a first
round. It won't hurt him to try. And someone
arranged for it on our behalf. We don't have to
worry about affording it . . ."

James couldn't feel his body. He couldn't feel
anything. He stared at Aunt Beth—then at the
guy in scrubs, who was watching them.

Aunt Beth noticed. "James, this is Andrew,
a special oncology nurse. He'll be overseeing
the treatment."

This was really happening. James struggled to take it in. "But you don't know who set this up? Or why?"

Why was he even asking? This had to be the Benefactor.

His aunt shook her head. "I may be able to find out more later. But for now I'm just grateful. Andrew thinks this will give Dad a real chance."

"It'll at least buy him some more time," said the nurse. "And honestly, Dr. Trudeleau, he's looking better already. The 30-percent statistic is very conservative. With continuing treatment, it's very possible he'll pull through . . ."

James had a hard time not whooping out loud. He settled for a grin instead.

Then he felt a buzz in his pocket. Andrew was talking to Beth about transfusions and bags and things. James took out the burner phone to read the text that had just come through.

> We know your grandfather is failing. We've arranged for one round of treatment for him. If you finish the contest, the money you win can provide the additional rounds of treatment he needs.

Relief flooded through James's body. And for the first time, he felt something like gratitude for the Benefactor.

Now he just needed to make sure his grandpa got the rest of the treatments he would need.

CHAPTER 18

TASK 8 COMPLETE

Your ninth task is to run away from home.
Leave a note for your family telling them not
to look for you or alert the police.

Your last task will be given to you tonight at
1:00 a.m. Go to 128 Nicollet Mall in downtown
Minneapolis. Wear the clothes you wore to
follow the man. Bring the phone. After this
task, you will receive a check for $10 million.

James stared at the computer. All his excitement,
all his renewed energy—gone. Replaced by anger.

This guy is just using Gramps to blackmail me. He has been all along. That's the only reason he wants to keep Gramps alive.

But it was working. James's grandpa was alive. And he was *so* close to being okay.

And James knew he couldn't give that up. No matter what the Benefactor asked of him now.

James tore a piece of paper from his notebook and scrawled: *I can't handle being here right now. I'm running away. Don't look for me, and don't call the police.* His pencil hovered over the page. Was he allowed to say anything more? What more *could* he say? He hoped the "right now" part would tell his aunt that he'd be coming back soon.

And it would be soon. As soon as he got the money tonight.

But then . . . if the Benefactor planned to give him the money right after the last task, why did James have to write this note? What was the point of telling his family he was running away? What did the Benefactor gain by making him do this?

James shook his head. Maybe the last task would take longer than the others. A few days, even. That had to be all it was. The Benefactor hadn't lied to him yet. He'd threatened him, pushed him, kept him in the dark—but he hadn't *lied*.

James left the note on his desk. He put on the clothes from the other night and slipped the burner phone into the jeans pocket. When he opened the door quietly, he could hear his aunt still talking to the nurse. "Come on into the kitchen, Andrew, the least I can do is offer you something to eat . . ." James slipped into his grandpa's room.

Maybe he was imagining it, but he thought his grandpa already looked better. More comfortable. More alert.

A smile came over the old man's face: James's favorite smile.

"How you feeling, old man?"

"Not so bad."

"You'll be back to your old self before you know it."

"I wouldn't bet on that, Doodle."

But I would, thought James. *I'm betting everything on that.*

James bent close and held his grandpa's hand. The lines of his hands were familiar and warm. They almost brought tears to James's eyes.

"Listen, Gramps . . ." He didn't know how to explain, but he knew he had to say something. He couldn't just disappear without a word—especially if he was going to be gone for a while. "I may be kind of busy for a few days. I might not be around. But—" He paused, weighing the words. The Benefactor seemed to hear everything, to know everything. James didn't dare say something the Benefactor didn't want him to. He couldn't risk being punished—or kicked out of the contest completely. Not this late in the game. "But it'll be OK," he said finally. "Just trust me. All right? Everything's going to be OK."

His grandpa squeezed his hand. "James," he said, "I am so proud of the man you have become."

The guilt rushed back, stronger than ever. But he couldn't afford that now. Not when he was this close. "Thanks, Gramps. You should probably rest now. I'll let you sleep."

James couldn't believe how hard it was to leave the room. To turn his back on his grandpa, not knowing when he'd be back. But it had to be soon. The Benefactor would keep Gramps alive until James finished the last task. And then James would have the money for the rest of the treatments. And everything would be fine.

That's what he kept telling himself as he walked out of the apartment.

* * * * *

A few minutes before 1:00 a.m., James stood outside the massive building at 128 Nicollet Mall. A guy bumped into him, someone his age, then said, "Sorry," and walked away quickly. James went back to staring up at the building. He put his hands in his coat pockets and was surprised to feel something inside one of them.

A white business-sized envelope. Who had put it there? Must've been the kid who bumped into him just now. He looked down the street but it was empty. On the front of the envelope was a handwritten message: "James. Sit on the bench at 1st and Nicollet." James scrunched up his face in confusion. This kept getting weirder and weirder.

He walked to a bench about half a block away and opened the note.

Dear James:

Congratulations! You have pleased us greatly. This last task is the most important one. Once you've completed it, your family will receive a check for $10 million. You can use this to continue your grandfather's treatment. We understand he is responding well so far.

Here is your task tonight: The security guards in the front lobby of this building will be called away at exactly 1:00 am. Take the elevator to the 15th floor. Use the map on the back of this letter to find the office of Jennifer McKnight. In her file cabinet, in drawer E–F, you will find a file labeled "EarthWatch Project Proposal." Take this file and leave the building.

When you exit the building, the guards may be back. Do whatever is necessary to get past them. Tools are provided under the bench seat.

After you exit, get into the white van waiting for you. The van will take you to your $10 million reward. Then you will be returned home.

Do not fail.

—The Benefactor

James reached under the bench and felt an object taped to the underside. He pulled and brought it up.

It was a gun.

One of those cowboy guns, the kind that people used for Russian Roulette. James started shaking. And just then the alarm he'd set on his phone went off: 1 a.m. He had to decide what to do with this thing.

He reread the letter. Turned it over and saw the floor map on the other side. With the weight of the gun in his hand, James couldn't push the questions back anymore. Who *were* they? Who was he working for?

This last task was beyond sketchy. Steal something, carry a gun, *get in a white van?* How was there any way that this was legit?

A picture of his grandpa filled his mind. Whoever was behind this had followed through on every promise so far, and then some. This was a well-planned contest. These people had power. James knew they would come through if he did this. He just had to make sure the guards wouldn't get hurt. He definitely couldn't and *wouldn't* shoot anyone. That was a deal breaker. If the Benefactor had other ideas, then that was too bad.

His grandpa had said he was proud of the man he'd become. Well, for the first time in a while, he would live up to that and follow his instincts. No gun.

James checked the chamber of the gun— carefully, trying to remember how he'd seen it done in movies. To his surprise, there were no bullets in there. Still, he didn't like the idea of even holding a gun, empty or not. And he couldn't just leave it here where someone else might find it . . .

Not knowing what else to do, he stood up and threw the gun in the garbage.

Then he squared his shoulders and walked to the building.

One more task.

CHAPTER 17

Sure enough, the guard desk was empty.

James ran to the elevators, punched the Up button, and got in as soon as a door slid open.

Inside the elevator, the button for the fifteenth floor was labeled "SolarStar." While the elevator rose, James looked at the map on the back of his letter, plotting a route to Jennifer McKnight's office. Once he stepped out onto the fifteenth floor, it was too dark to see much. But he didn't dare turn on any overhead lights. Instead he tried to remember the floor's layout.

Squinting at a name plate in the dark, he found Jennifer McKnight's office. The door was unlocked, so he tiptoed in. He went straight to the file cabinet, which opened easily.

James worked as fast as he could, looking through files by the light of his phone screen. *Prototypes in Development. EarthWatch Development Minutes. Manufacturing Research.*

He remembered Sandra Bravo's work at EarthWatch. Could that be related to the project proposal he was about to steal? SolarStar was clearly tied to EarthWatch. But why did that matter to the Benefactor? This whole contest couldn't possibly be about something as harmless as solar power, could it? *No time—keep going.* He flipped through the files faster.

Suddenly a flashlight beam swept the floor near the office door. James bit back a curse. He'd left the door open. Genius.

He shoved the drawer closed and ducked behind the desk. Out in the hall, he could hear two men talking.

"These idiots don't lock their offices. Look at this. This one is wide open. I'm tempted to steal something just to teach them a lesson."

The other man laughed. "Nothing here worth stealing. Gotta love the nonprofit world." James saw footsteps near the door.

The door to the office closed. James heard, muffled, "These rounds are hard on my old bones. But this is what they pay us for, huh?"

James heard a grunt far away. After that the security guards' voices disappeared. He counted to a hundred, then stood up on wobbly legs, opened the door, and peeked out. No one. The light from the hallway shone through the door on the cabinet.

James lunged back to the E–F drawer. And there it was. *EarthWatch Project Proposal.* Now all James had to do was get out. If the guards were on their rounds, checking every floor, he had plenty of time.

He closed the door to the office and raced toward the elevators. Then he stopped. What if he ran into the guards? He should take the stairs instead . . .

He found the door to the stairway and jogged down the steps. Every squeak of his sneakers seemed to echo through the stairwell.

When he got to the first floor, he opened the door quietly and looked out. No guards. He headed for the front door.

A voice called out, "What do you think you're doing here? Stop right there!"

James froze and turned around. *Where did he come from?*

A gray-haired, white security guard pointed a Taser at him. James thanked his lucky stars that it wasn't a gun. And that he'd had the sense to get rid of the Benefactor's gun. James put his hands out to the side, one palm open and the other holding the file. He didn't dare make another move.

The guard spoke into a walkie-talkie he held with his other hand, keeping his eye on James. "Yeah, I got a break-in here. I need backup. Young black male, six-one."

Then he looked James right in the eye and said into the set, "Suspect is armed."

CHAPTER 18

Fury ran through James. Then fear. Then fury again. His hands were open. It was clear he wasn't armed.

James wanted nothing more than to lunge at this guy and punch him in the face, Taser or not. But then he heard his grandpa's voice in his head again.

So instead he said as calmly as he could, "Sir, I'm not armed. I'm sorry, I know I shouldn't be here. I took this file. I would be happy to give it back to you."

"Don't move!" the guard shouted. From somewhere outside, James heard sirens far away. He began to shake. This was the scariest moment of his life. The security guard raised the Taser and stepped forward.

From out of nowhere, a can bounced into the lobby, leaking gas. James's eyes started to tear up and he couldn't see. Someone grabbed his jacket roughly and pulled him out onto the street.

James felt the night air hit him. He still couldn't see.

A voice whispered in his ear. "Come on, we have to get out of here!"

James followed the voice, breaking into a run. He squinted through stinging eyes and got a glimpse of the person in front of him.

Brown hair streamed behind her. And when she turned around, he recognized those eyes. He almost stopped running.

It was Ana.

ABOUT THE AUTHOR

Megan Atwood lives and works in Minneapolis, Minnesota, where she teaches creative writing at a local college and the Loft Literary Center. She has an MFA in writing for children and young adults and was a 2009 Artist Initiative grant recipient through the Minnesota State Arts Board. She has been published in literary and academic journals and has the best cat that has ever lived.